Copyright © 1999 by Nord-Süd Verlag AG, Gossau Zürich, Switzerland
First published in Switzerland under the title *August und das rote Ding*
English translation copyright © 1999 by North-South Books Inc.
All rights reserved.
No part of this book may be reproduced or utilized in any form
or by any means, electronic or mechanical, including photocopying,
recording, or any information storage and retrieval system,
without permission in writing from the publisher.
First published in the United States, Great Britain, Canada,
Australia, and New Zealand in 1999 by North-South Books,
an imprint of Nord-Süd Verlag AG, Gossau Zürich, Switzerland.
Distributed in the United States by North-South Books Inc., New York.
Library of Congress Cataloging-in-Publication Data is available.
A CIP catalogue record for this book is available from The British Library.
ISBN 0-7358-1168-7 (trade binding)
1 3 5 7 9 TB 10 8 6 4 2
ISBN 0-7358-1169-5 (library binding)
1 3 5 7 9 LB 10 8 6 4 2
Printed in Belgium
For more information about our books,
and the authors and artists who create them,
visit our web site: http://www.northsouth.com

The Circus of Mystery

WRITTEN AND ILLUSTRATED BY

Maura Fazzi and Peter Kühner

Translated by Rosemary Lanning

North-South Books

New York / London

At last, amid all the grey,
something bright and shiny!
It was a round, red nose.
It looked out of place.
Augustus felt out of place, too,
at the back of the faceless crowd.
He stooped to pick up
the red nose, and put it on.

Augustus admired
his reflection in a shop
window, and smiled
at himself.
He was a clown!

Everything around him brightened.
A rainbow spanned the sky, and
a tightrope walker skipped across it.
Augustus felt dizzy.
A sunbeam tickled him,
and he had to sneeze.
The red nose flew off.

Suddenly everything was grey again.

Augustus stumbled
after the red nose.
He found it in the
subway and put it
back on. Things
looked brighter
again, and the
tightrope walker
was back. She
followed him,
smiling.

Augustus strolled along  cracking jokes, playing tricks,   and making friends.

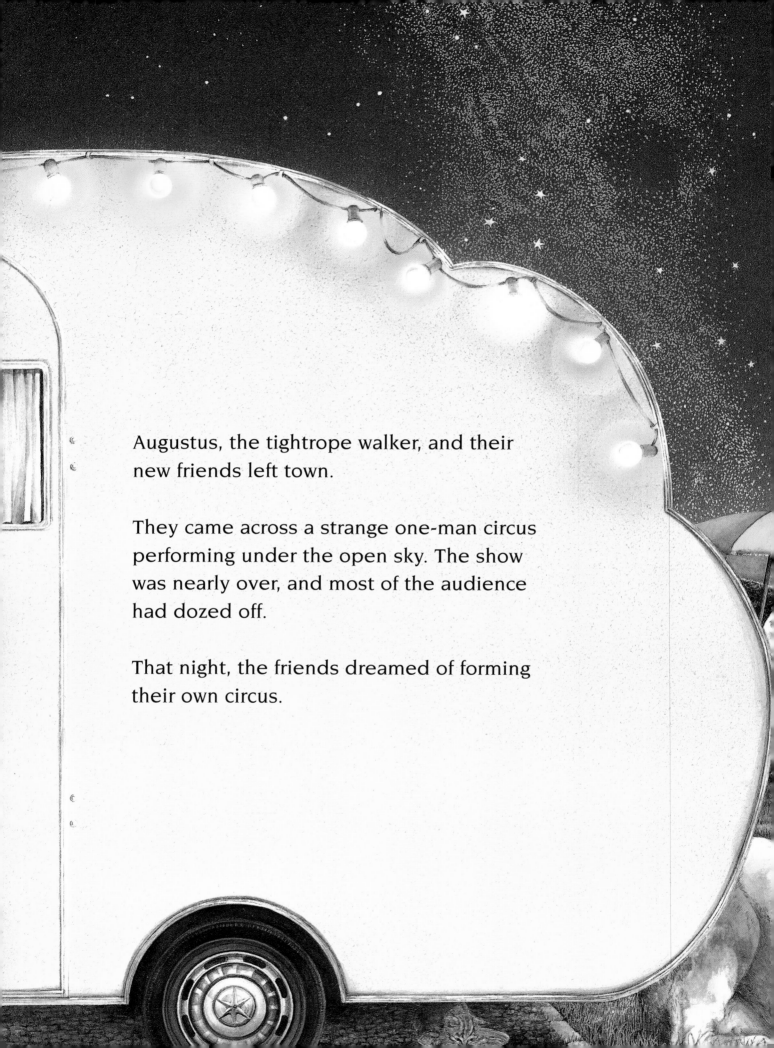

Augustus, the tightrope walker, and their
new friends left town.

They came across a strange one-man circus
performing under the open sky. The show
was nearly over, and most of the audience
had dozed off.

That night, the friends dreamed of forming
their own circus.

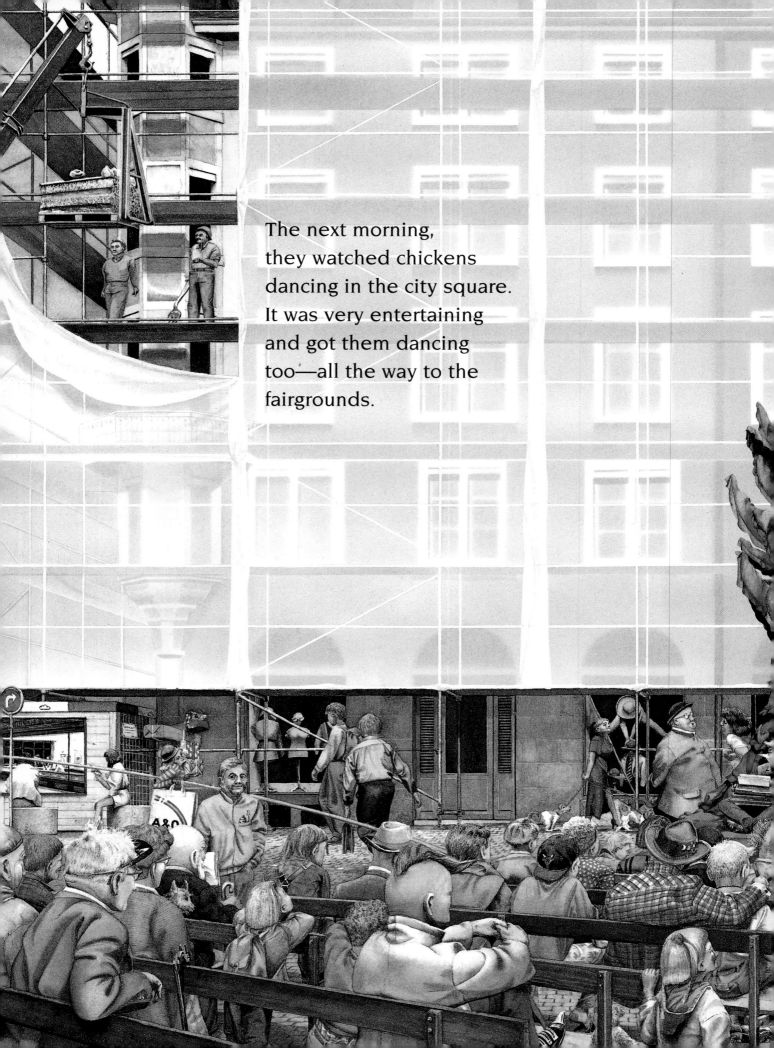

The next morning,
they watched chickens
dancing in the city square.
It was very entertaining
and got them dancing
too—all the way to the
fairgrounds.

In the middle of the fairgrounds stood a lost boy.
He was crying. Augustus went to comfort him.
"Try this," he said, and gave him the red nose.

When the boy saw his reflection in a puddle, he laughed.
That reminded the friends of their circus dream.
They hurried off to the scrapyard.

In the scrapyard
were hundreds of weird,
wonderful things
they could use.

They chose a bathtub,
an old stove,
a trunk for costumes,
and a huge canvas elephant.

Now their rehearsals could begin. They had dancers, jugglers, and a bathtub full of soap for blowing rainbow-striped bubbles.

At last everything was ready.
"Welcome, ladies and gentlemen!"
called Augustus.
"Step this way, boys and girls!
The fun is about to begin!"

It was a spectacular show!

And to think—it all started
with a small, round,
red nose.